Poland

Denise Allard

RSVP

**RAINTREE
STECK-VAUGHN**
P U B L I S H E R S
The Steck-Vaughn Company

Austin, Texas

Published by Raintree Steck-Vaughn Publishers, an imprint of Steck-Vaughn Company

A ZOË BOOK

Editor: Kath Davies, Pam Wells
Design: Sterling Associates
Map: Julian Baker
Production: Grahame Griffiths

Library of Congress Cataloging-in-Publication Data

Allard, Denise. 1952-
    Poland / Denise Allard.
        p. cm. — (Postcards from)
    "A Zoë Book"—Verso t.p.
    Includes index.
    Summary: A collection of fictional postcards, written as if by young people visiting Poland, describing various sights and ways of life in this northern European country.
    ISBN 0-8172-4025-X (hardcover). — ISBN 0-8172-6208-3 (softcover)
    1. Poland—Description and travel—Juvenile literature. [1. Poland—Description and travel. 2. Postcards.] I. Title. II. Series.
DK4081. A44 1997
914.3804'56—dc20   95–53804
                                                      CIP
                                                      AC

Printed and bound in the United States
1 2 3 4 5 6 7 8 9 0 WZ 99 98 97 96

Photographic acknowledgments

The publishers wish to acknowledge, with thanks, the following photographic sources:

Adina Tovy - cover tl; / Gavin Hellier 6; / Robert Harding Picture Library; The Hutchison Library / Christina Dodwell 24; / Impact Photos / Rupert Conant - cover bl, 8, 26; / Anne-Marie Purkiss - title page, 20, 28; / Peter Arkell 10; / Alain Le Garsmeur 12; / John Denham 18; Zefa - cover r, 14, 16, 22.

The publishers have made every effort to trace the copyright holders, but if they have inadvertently overlooked any, they will be pleased to make the necessary arrangement at the first opportunity.

Contents

All the words that appear in **bold** are
explained in the Glossary on page 30.

N

| 0 | 100 miles |
| 0 | 200 km |

Sweden

Baltic Sea

Lithuania

Gdansk

Russia

•Swinoujscie

Masuria

Vistula River

Belarus

Poznan

Warsaw■

Germany

Poland

Mount Snezka
▲ (5,259ft.)

Sudeten Mountains

Krakow

Zakopane

Ukraine

Czech Republic

Slovakia

Austria

Hungary

The World

A big map of Poland
and a small map of the world

Dear Rob,

You can see Poland in red on the small map. It is shaped like a square. The plane took over seven hours to get here from Boston. The weather here is like the weather at home.

Love,

Wendy

P.S. We flew across the Atlantic Ocean and over many countries to get here. Mom says that Poland is much smaller than the United States.

The Old Town, Warsaw

Dear Tanya,

We are in Warsaw. It is the **capital** city of Poland. Our hotel is in the new part of Warsaw. We went for a ride around the Old Town in a cart pulled by a horse.

Yours,

Tom

P.S. Mom says that bombs destroyed most of the buildings here during the last **war**. Many buildings were rebuilt. But they look like the ones that were destroyed.

Sunday lunch in Poland

Dear Sally,

We love the food in Poland.
I like roast potatoes best.
Sometimes we go to a café.
We have a cup of tea and
some cupcakes. Mom pays for
our meals with Polish money,
called *zlotys*.

Your friend,

Larry

P.S. Mom likes the candy, but my brother
wants to eat hot dogs all the time. Luckily
we can buy them here.

A boat trip on the Vistula River

Dear Bruce,

The Vistula River runs through
the middle of Poland. It is
Poland's longest river. We went
on a boat trip from Warsaw.
The riverboat sailed along
the Vistula toward the city
of Krakow.

Your friend,

Wesley

P.S. Dad says that we are going on another
boat trip next week. We are going to Masuria,
where there are lots of lakes.

Buses, cars, and streetcars in Warsaw

Dear Natasha,

Most people in Poland do not own a car. They travel around by bus. There are plenty of buses. They go all over the country. For long distances, people often travel by train.

Love,

Kim

P.S. Not many people in Poland speak English. Most people only speak Polish. I like to sit on the bus and listen to people talking. They speak very fast.

Old buildings in Krakow

Dear Jan,

We are staying in the city of Krakow. The old town is more than 1,000 years old. We visited a **museum**, and then we went shopping. I bought a Polish doll.

See you soon,

Sholeh

P.S. We went to see some salt **mines**. They were not far from Krakow. The mines were huge. We could walk around inside. Dad says that miners had a very hard life.

Mountain dogs pulling a sleigh at
Zakopane

Dear José,

I wish we could come here in the winter. I want to ride on a sleigh. We are in southwest Poland. We have come here to walk in the mountains and forests.

Your friend,

Alice

P.S. Mom says that the Sudeten Mountains are on the border with a country called the Czech Republic. The highest mountain is Mount Snezka.

Musicians playing in Krakow

Dear Linda,

Polish people try to remember the past. They believe that it is important to do this. They like to wear **traditional** clothes. They play Polish music and sing Polish songs.

Love,

Kathy

P.S. We went to a museum in the city of Poznan. It was full of musical instruments. Dad says that Poland is famous for making musical instruments.

A beach on the Baltic coast

Dear Alex,

We spent today on the beach. Our vacation cottage looks out onto the Baltic Sea. There are lots of people here. They are enjoying the fresh air and the sunshine.

Your friend,

Ben

P.S. The city of Swinoujscie is not far from here. Mom says that it is a busy **port**. Boats take people and goods across the Baltic Sea to Germany and Denmark.

The old port at Gdansk

Dear Rich,

Gdansk is the largest city in the north of Poland. It has been a port for hundreds of years. There is a huge wooden **crane** here that is about 500 years old.

Your friend,

David

P.S. Dad says that Gdansk is still an important port. Ships are loaded with Polish goods that are sold all over the world. They also build large ships here.

Polish dancers in traditional dress

Dear Anna,

Polish people love to sing and to dance. Children learn traditional songs and dances in school. They play other sports and games at school.

Your friend,

Mike

P.S. Dad says that Polish people like walking. There are many good trails to follow. Sailing and canoeing are popular, too. In winter, people go skiing in the mountains.

Lighting candles on All Souls' Day

Dear Juanita,

This is a special day when **Christians** remember people who have died. They light candles for them. Most people in Poland are Christians. They belong to the **Roman Catholic** Church.

Your sister,

Maria

P.S. Mom says that this is part of a Christian **festival**. There are many different festivals in Poland.

The Polish flag flying in Warsaw

Dear Erica,

The Polish flag has two stripes. The top one is white, and the bottom one is red. Red and white have been Poland's colors for more than 700 years.

Love,

Rosa

P.S. Mom says that people in Poland choose their own leaders. Poland is a **republic**. The head of the country is called the president. This way of ruling is called a **democracy**.

Glossary

Capital: The town or city where people who rule the country meet

Christians: People who follow the teachings of Jesus. Jesus lived about 2,000 years ago.

Crane: A machine that lifts and moves heavy objects

Democracy: A country where the people choose the leaders they want to run the country

Festival: A time when people remember something special that happened in the past

Mine: A place where something such as coal, gold, or salt is dug out. Mines are often deep under the ground.

Museum: A building where interesting things from the past are on display

Port: A town or city where ships are loaded or unloaded with goods. People sometimes travel on ships, called ferries, from ports.

P.S.: This stands for Post Script. A postscript is the part of a card or letter that is added at the end, after the person has signed it.

Republic: A country where the people choose their leaders. A republic does not have a king or a queen.

Roman Catholic: One of many Christian faiths. The Pope is the leader of the Roman Catholic Church.

Traditional: Doing something in the same way that people have in the past. Young people learn how to do this from older people.

War: A time when groups of people, from different places or countries, fight each other

Index